To Kimmi, Ari, Milo, Mom, Dad, Rebecca,
Josh, Gracie, Farfel, and all fun dogs!
—E.T.B.

For my dogs, Rosie and George,
who will probably never read this
—J.C.

All rights reserved. Published in the United States by Random House Children's Books,
a division of Penguin Random House LLC, New York.

Random House and the colophon are registered trademarks of Penguin Random House LLC.

Visit us on the Web! rhcbooks.com

Educators and librarians, for a variety of teaching tools, visit us at RHTeachersLibrarians.com

Library of Congress Cataloging-in-Publication Data
Names: Berlin, Ethan T., author. | Chapman, Jared, illustrator.
Title: I am not a dog toy / by Ethan T. Berlin ; illustrated by Jared Chapman.
Description: First edition. | New York : Random House Children's Books, [2021] | Audience: Ages 3–7. | Audience: Grades K–1. |
Summary: "A stuffed bear looking for a best friend believes he is meant to be a child's toy,
but true friendship comes to him from a place he least expects." —Provided by publisher.
Identifiers: LCCN 2019051697 (print) | LCCN 2019051698 (ebook)
ISBN 978-0-593-11901-3 (hardcover) | ISBN 978-0-593-11902-0 (library binding) | ISBN 978-0-593-11903-7 (ebook)
Subjects: CYAC: Teddy bears—Fiction. | Dogs—Fiction. | Humorous stories.
Classification: LCC PZ7.1.B458 Iam 2021 (print) | LCC PZ7.1.B458 (ebook) | DDC [E]—dc23

The artist set up his studio in a kennel to create the illustrations.
Book design by Nicole de las Heras

MANUFACTURED IN CHINA
10 9 8 7 6 5 4 3 2 1
First Edition

I AM NOT A DOG TOY

written by
Ethan T. Berlin

illustrated by
Jared Chapman

Random House 🏠 New York

Hello!
I'm going to be your most
favorite toy ever!

Yeah. I'm gonna put you over here.

Hello! You're going to be my most favorite toy ever!

That is such a unique offer.
But I am not a dog toy.

Dog toys are torn-up,
disgusting things that
weren't good enough
to be kids' toys.

And I am a fancy kids' toy
with lots of pockets.

Wasn't that the most fun ever?
You're totally a dog toy!

First, that was not the most fun ever!
Second, that was so much fun!
And third, I am not a dog toy!

See, here comes my best
friend, a kid, to rescue me
from you, a dog.

What is this thing
doing on my bed?!

I AM A KIDS' TOY!

And this kid
is going to play with me!

Let's fight some bad guys!

Let's ride around in circles!

SHOVE!

Let's make the biggest fort ever!

BUMP

Having fun?

No! This kid is
so boring!

Maybe you should consider playing
with a really fun dog.

No, no, no!
I'm supposed to be a kids' toy!

I'm going to find someone who wants to be my best friend. Someone who likes to fight bad guys and build forts and fight different bad guys!

Someone who thinks it's really cool that I have so many pockets!

Someone who is fun to play with and would never put me in the wedge.

Someone who is . . .

Let's run around in circles!

I AM
A DOG TOY,
AND IT IS
GLORIOUS!